because of Misha and for Jack

This book was created with India ink on vellum and colored digitally.

Library of Congress Control Number 2022932877

ISBN 978-1-4197-5894-2

Text and illustrations © 2023 Charlie Mylie
Book design by Heather Kelly

Published in 2023 by Abrams Appleseed, an imprint of ABRAMS. All rights reserved.
No portion of this book may be reproduced, stored in a retrieval system, or transmitted in any form or
by any means, mechanical, electronic, photocopying, recording, or otherwise,
without written permission from the publisher.

Abrams Appleseed is a registered trademark of Harry N. Abrams, Inc.

Printed and bound in China
10 9 8 7 6 5 4 3 2 1

For bulk discount inquiries, contact specialsales@abramsbooks.com.

ABRAMS The Art of Books
195 Broadway, New York, NY 10007
abramsbooks.com

WE MIGHT SEE

charlie mylie

abrams appleseed   new york

LOOKING UP IN THE SKY,

plane

I LOVE YOU

day

cloud

balloon

tower

crane

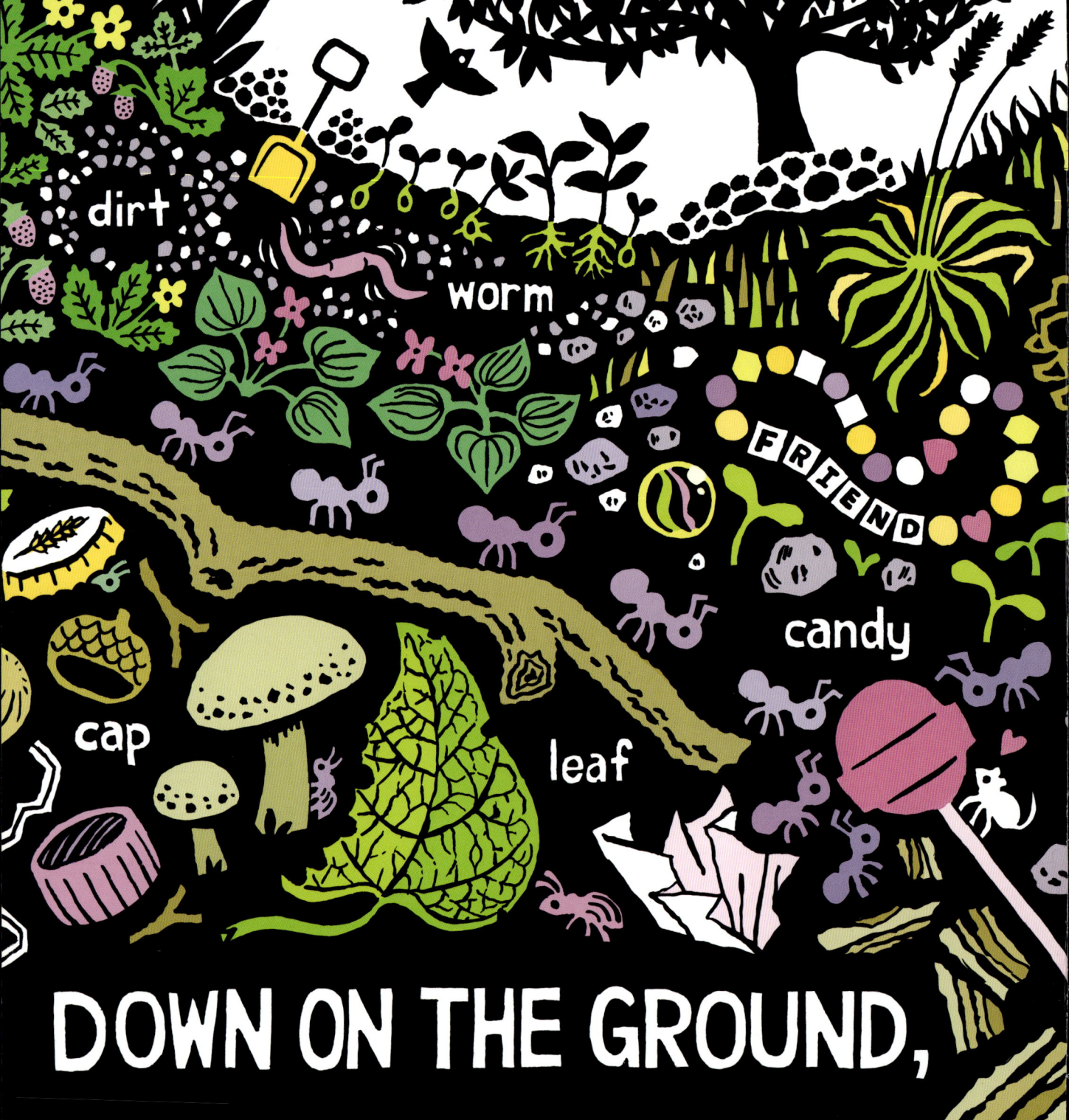

A CHANCE TO SAY "REMEMBER TODAY?"

 playing
 jumping
 sharing
 digging
 growing

trying flying

tasting

smelling listening

singing

CLOSING OUR EYES,